The Seal Mother
› MORDICAI GERSTEIN ‹

Dial Books for Young Readers : New York

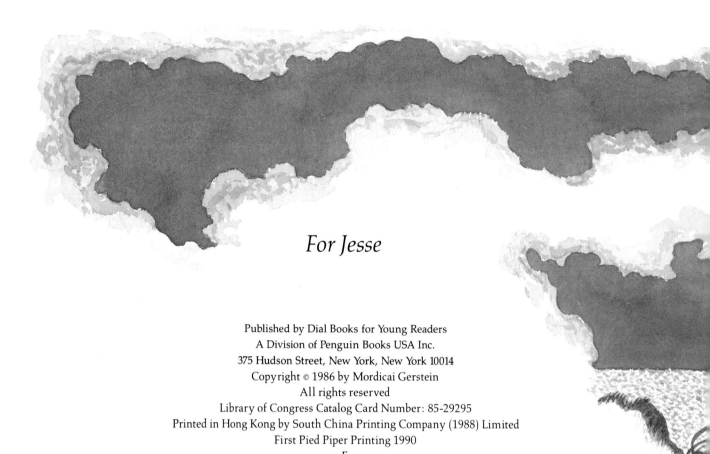

For Jesse

Published by Dial Books for Young Readers
A Division of Penguin Books USA Inc.
375 Hudson Street, New York, New York 10014
Copyright © 1986 by Mordicai Gerstein
All rights reserved
Library of Congress Catalog Card Number: 85-29295
Printed in Hong Kong by South China Printing Company (1988) Limited
First Pied Piper Printing 1990
E
3 5 7 9 10 8 6 4 2

A Pied Piper Book is a registered trademark of
Dial Books for Young Readers,
a division of Penguin Books USA, Inc.,
® TM 1,163,686 and ® TM 1,054,312.

THE SEAL MOTHER
is published in a hardcover edition by
Dial Books for Young Readers.
ISBN 0-8037-0743-6

The Seal Mother is based on a Scottish folktale that is known
to be several centuries old. Various versions of the tale
have appeared in English folklore collections
and were the inspiration for this original telling.

The full-color artwork was prepared in watercolor and gouache.
It was then color-separated and reproduced
in red, blue, yellow, and black halftones.

On a little island in the North Atlantic an old man sits by
the sea and plays a fiddle in the long twilight of Midsummer's Eve.
The seals sing on the rocks in the bay. They sound almost human
and seem to sing along with the old man's fiddle.

If you should happen to be there and hear this strange wild music, walk up to the old man and wish him good evening. Then politely ask why he's fiddling there and if the seals are really singing with him.

He'll look at you a moment. You'll notice that his eyes are large, dark, and deep. He'll light his pipe and if he decides he likes you, he'll say, "Sit down, it's a long story."

Accept his invitation and sit beside him. This is what he'll tell you.

It was on a moonlit Midsummer's Eve like this one, about a hundred years ago, that a fisherman out on these waters saw a wondrous thing.

As he watched, a seal clambered out of the water onto a tiny
rock island. It shook itself dry, and after basking a moment in the
moonlight, it began to wriggle out of its skin.

The skin fell away like an old robe and out stepped the most beautiful woman the fisherman had ever seen. He nearly tumbled out of his boat. In that first moment he fell completely in love.

The seal woman didn't see him. She folded her skin neatly and set it aside. Then she stretched and twirled and began to dance, singing and laughing in the moonlight. The fisherman let his boat drift close. He found the sealskin and hid it under his nets.

Then, gathering his courage, he stepped up to the woman and asked her to marry him. She appeared startled. Then she said, "You seem a sincere and handsome man, but I am a seal. My home and people are in the sea, and I prefer to stay there, thank you."

 With lowered eyes the fisherman told the woman that he'd
taken her skin.

 "Give it back!" she demanded. "Without it I can't turn back into
a seal." Her deep, dark eyes flashed with anger.

 "Dear lady, forgive me!" cried the fisherman on his knees.
"If you marry me, I'll give you back your skin after seven years.
Then you can stay or go as you wish. That is my solemn promise."

The woman looked at him unhappily.

"If that is true," she said at last, "then I will marry you."

As the fisherman rowed them home, he was so happy he thought he might fly. He didn't hear the sad song the woman sang. Nor did he see the great gray seal that followed them and sang just as sadly.

They were married and it wasn't long before they had a little
boy. They named him Andrew.

"He has his mother's eyes," said all the uncles and aunts. No
one guessed that Andrew's mother was a seal, not even Andrew.
His father had hidden the sealskin carefully in a little cave on
the far side of their island.

As soon as Andrew was big enough, he went out fishing
with his father. The boy loved the sea, and they always had fun
together and brought home lots of fish.

In the evenings while his father played the fiddle Andrew's mother told stories of a world beneath the sea.

"For everything on land," she said, "there is a similar thing in the sea. There are birds and cows of the sea. There are mountains and trees and cities of the sea."

"Are there people?" the boy asked.

"Yes," answered his mother. "They are the seals."

"They are the animals most like humans. And there is a kind of seal called a selkie. On Midsummer's Eve, the longest night of the year, the selkies take human form to dance and sing. They love music."

"How do you know all this?" Andrew asked her.

"Never mind!" cried Andrew's father, putting down his fiddle. "It's late, and there are fish to catch in the morning."

It was on a Midsummer's Eve that Andrew woke past midnight and heard his parents' voices.

"The seven years have passed," said his mother. "You must give me my sealskin."

"Will you stay or will you leave us?" asked his father.

"I must have my sealskin first, as you promised," replied his mother. "When I have it, I'll tell you."

"Then I can't give it to you," said his father. "I won't risk your leaving our son without a mother."

"It was your solemn promise!" Andrew's mother said, but his father didn't answer. Andrew heard him putting on his boots and slicker. The door slammed, and then there was only the sound of his mother sobbing.

Andrew lay in his bed wide-eyed and frightened. What did it mean? he wondered. What was the sealskin? Why would his mother ever leave him?

Just before dawn Andrew woke again and heard a beautiful
voice singing. It seemed to call to him. "Andrew! Andrew!"
    He slipped out of bed and tiptoed past his mother who was
asleep at the table. The song drew him over the fields to the
far side of the island.

There, on a rock beyond the surf, a great gray seal sat singing. Thinking to climb down to the water, Andrew looked over the edge of the cliff. He saw a small cave. He crawled in and found a bundle wrapped in oilcloth and tied with fishing line. He opened it carefully.

Inside there was a velvety gray sealskin, neatly folded. When
he held it up, he felt as if his mother were there with him.

It's the one they fought about! thought Andrew.

He was trembling. Somehow this sealskin could cause his mother
to leave him. That must be why his father had hidden it there.

Yet it's hers and she needs it! thought Andrew. He promised it
to her!

Andrew was frightened and confused. He didn't know what
to do.

Then he heard the seal once again and realized he understood its song. He jumped up and listened.

My daughter is a bonny seal. She was born beneath the sea.
But till she has her sealskin back, she will a prisoner be.
She's a woman on the land. She's a selkie in the sea.
But without her own true sealskin, she never can be free.

Without another thought Andrew took the skin and ran all the way home.

He woke his mother and put the skin on her lap.

"My dearest boy!" she said, and her eyes filled with tears.

"Whatever happens now, you must trust me and not be afraid."

"I promise," said Andrew.

She took the skin and ran with Andrew down to the cliff.

    At the very edge of the cliff, Andrew's mother put on the skin and he saw her become a beautiful gray seal. Then she embraced him and blew into his mouth, filling his lungs with air. Holding him tight, she dove off the cliff and into the sea.

She dove deep, and the boy saw rayfish and squid flash by.
He saw fish that looked like birds and fish that looked like cows
and horses.

They left the sun behind and in the dim waters he saw trees and mountains and crystal cities lit with phosphorus.

They swam upward and the water grew brighter.

They burst into the air in a cove of white rock. There were
seals everywhere.

"This is your seal family," said Andrew's mother. "For as you
now know, I am a selkie."

"Yes," said Andrew, "and I am part seal."

They climbed onto the rocks and the great gray seal came to
meet them.

"This is my father," said Andrew's mother. "He is your seal grandfather."

"It was he who led me to your skin." said Andrew. The seal embraced them warmly. Then Andrew's seal uncles and aunts, and his seal cousins came to meet and embrace them too.

"And now," said his mother with tears in her eyes, "you must
go back to your father. He is a good man and he loves you.
You are part human, but I am a seal. I must stay with my people.
Whenever you want to visit me, sing out on the cliffs and one
of the family will come for you."

"I'll come often," sobbed Andrew.

They kissed and parted sadly. Andrew rode home on the back
of an uncle.

When Andrew told his father what had happened the poor
man sat down and wept.

"It's my own fault," he said over and over. "I should never have
forced her to stay with me."

Andrew visited his mother often as he was growing up. He became a fisherman like his father and always caught plenty of fish. The seals saw to that.

He married a lovely young woman and it wasn't long before they had lots of children.

Every Midsummer's Eve, Andrew rowed his family out to a tiny rock island in the sea.

The seals met them there, and they danced and laughed and sang together all night long.

At the end of his story the old man will pause, look at you with his deep, dark eyes, and he'll wink.

"And I am one of that family," he'll continue, "and tonight is Midsummer's Eve."

The old man will stand and wave to people who are coming down the beach to meet him. They'll be singing and laughing and carrying boats and oars, fiddles, whistles, and drums. The seals will sing and dive around the rocks.

And if the old man should say to you, as he pushes his boat into the surf, "Would you care to join us?"

Take my advice, say, "Yes!"